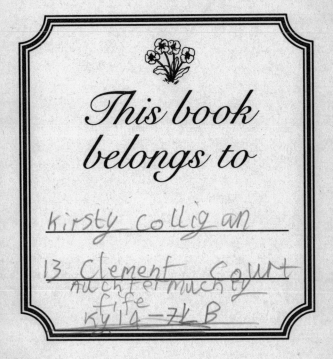

This book belongs to

Kirsty Colligan

13 Clement Court
Auchtermuchty
Fife
KY14 - 7LB

The
Forgetful
Squirrel
AND OTHER WOODLAND STORIES

The
Forgetful
Squirrel

AND OTHER WOODLAND STORIES

First published in Great Britain in 1998 by
Parragon
13 Whiteladies Road
Clifton
Bristol BS8 1PB

ISBN 0 75252-535-2

Printed in Great Britain

Produced by Nicola Baxter
PO Box 71 Diss Norfolk IP22 2DT

Stories by Nicola Baxter, except
Good Neighbours by Ronne Randall
Designed by Amanda Hawkes
Text illustrations by Duncan Gutteridge
Cover illustration by Alisa Tingley

Contents

The Forgetful Squirrel

Snow glittered on the branches of the trees in Southfield Wood. Their leaves had long ago fallen, and the bare bark looked cold and grey beneath its white frosting. Down on the woodland floor, nothing moved except the occasional brown shrivelled leaf, drifting across the moss in the light breeze. The only sound was the sighing of the breeze and the far-off barking of a hungry fox.

High in the branches of an oak tree, the little squirrel slept soundly. She could not really hear the fox's cry, but still, in her sleep, she rolled herself into an even tighter, furry ball and tucked her little paws under her chin. She had made herself a cosy nest of twigs and leaves, as round as a ball. Inside, she was safe from the cold winds and the drifting snow.

The squirrel had been asleep since the first really cold day of winter. Once or twice, on a very sunny day, her little nose had twitched, and she had peeped out of her nest, or drey. But it was always too cold to go hunting for something to eat. Besides, she had spent the summer and autumn filling her tummy with all her favourite foods, so that she would be able to sleep through the winter without a single dinner.

The little squirrel slept on through the cold months. Elsewhere in the wood, other little creatures were fast asleep as well. Meanwhile, underground, the first stirrings of life began as tiny shoots started to make their long journey to the surface.

At last there came a day when the sunshine was quite warm on the branches. The snow had long ago melted away, and the sky had changed from grey to a watery blue.

The next day, the sun was even warmer, and it shone for a few minutes longer. Spring was well and truly on its way.

In her cosy drey, the little squirrel stirred. She felt the warmth of the sun trickling through the twigs and leaves of her treetop home. And she felt, too, that her tummy was just a tiny bit empty.

Poking her nose through the bottom of her nest, the little squirrel looked around at the waking world.

Far below, the first green shoots were showing under the trees. A few little animals were scurrying about among the roots and moss. The little squirrel wondered what she could find to eat so early in the year. Then she remembered something very important. Many months ago, when the nut-trees had been bowed down with shiny brown nuts, she had gathered dozens and dozens of them and stored them away for a morning just like this.

With a little chuckle, the squirrel clambered out of her nest and ran lightly along the branch. When it came to tree-climbing, she was an expert. Her clever little paws grasped the branches, while her big furry tail helped her to balance as she

leapt without hesitation from branch to branch. However high she climbed, the little squirrel felt no fear. The treetops were her home, and she was happy there.

But the little squirrel had not hidden her nuts in the treetops. She had dug several little holes in the ground and buried her store here and there in the forest. Now all she had to do was to find one of these stores and enjoy her first meal of the year.

The little squirrel skipped happily down the trunk of the tree and looked around. She knew that one of her secret hiding places was not very far.

But, oh dear, how different things looked after the winter snows. The little squirrel remembered that her store was near a small bush with bright red and orange leaves. But now the leaves had all disappeared. Every bush was a mass of bare twigs. It was impossible to tell them apart.

Then the little squirrel remembered something else. There had been some red and white spotted toadstools near her hiding place. She looked eagerly around, but the clump of toadstools had also disappeared.

For the first time, the little squirrel began to feel worried. What if she couldn't find any of her nuts? What would she eat? How could she survive until spring had properly arrived?

All too soon, the light began to fade. Knowing that it would soon be cold and dark, the little squirrel hurried back to her home, where she could curl up, warm and safe, until morning.

"I'll worry about where my nut-store is then," she said to herself. "Tonight I will have a good sleep, so that I am ready to search tomorrow."

But in the morning, the little squirrel had no more idea where she had stored her food than she had had the night before.

"Perhaps I will be able to see where the ground has been disturbed," thought the little squirrel. But even as the thought crossed her mind, she recalled vividly how carefully she had patted the earth back into place after each burial.

"I have been *too* clever," said the little squirrel. "What am I going to do?"

All day long, the hungry creature scampered through the wood. She was so worried about her food-stores now that she was not very careful to look out for danger. That is why, as she bounded around the base of a mighty oak tree, she came face to face with a long, lean, reddish creature. It was the fox!

Now foxes do not often catch squirrels, for they are not good climbers, but no hungry fox is going to give up the chance of supper when it comes leaping towards him. With one swift movement, the fox caught hold of the little squirrel's tail in his strong jaws.

"Where are you off to?" he asked between clenched teeth.

"I'm … I'm … I'm searching for my food-stores," said the little squirrel in a rush. The poor little animal was so frightened that she said the first thing that came into her head, which happened to be the truth.

"Food-stores?" queried the fox, for at least one of those words was of very great interest to him at the moment. "And what might be in these food-stores?"

"Oh, um, rabbits," said the squirrel, thinking as fast as she could. "Rabbits and chickens and one or two ducks."

The very mention of those creatures made the fox's mouth water. They were much more to his liking than squirrel, which in fact he had never tasted.

"And where exactly are these food-stores?" he enquired.

The little squirrel had her wits about her now.

"They are here somewhere," she said. "But I can't quite remember which tree I hid them under. It will take me weeks to find them, but with your strong paws and digging expertise, you will be able to unearth them in a few minutes. I think that this tree is the best place to start."

The fox had begun digging before he had even had a chance to think about what the squirrel had said. Somehow the mention of chickens and rabbits and ducks had muddled his usually sharp brain.

The digging was much slower than usual because the fox had

to keep a tight grip on the squirrel's tail, but before long he had dug quite a deep hole under the oak tree.

There was nothing there at all.

"Then it might be this tree," said the squirrel, pointing to a nearby trunk.

The fox felt that he had very little to lose. After all, if he did not find the food-store, at least he had a plump little squirrel for his supper.

But the second hole was empty as well.

"One more," growled the fox between his teeth, "and then I'm going to eat you!"

The fox began to dig his third hole, and it did not take him long to come upon a whole mass of little round, brown shiny objects.

The fox could not believe his eyes. He felt a great anger rising up inside him and he opened his mouth in a mighty shout.

"NUTS?" he bellowed. "What good are nuts to ME?"

But, of course, when he opened his mouth, the little squirrel was able to jump free, and in ten seconds flat, she had scampered to the top of the nearest tree.

"They're terribly good for you!" she called down cheekily. "A nut a day keeps the doctor away, that's what I always say."

The fox was absolutely furious. He chased his tail round and round the tree to relieve his feelings. Then he sat down to wait with a very determined expression on his foxy face.

"Little squirrel," he called, "I'm going to wait here until you come down. You can't stay up there for ever."

"No," called the squirrel, "but I can jump to another tree, just look at me!" And spreading her beautiful tail out behind her, she leapt across the clearing to the tree opposite.

Now, the fox could not sit at the bottom of every tree in the wood, and anyway, his tummy, which had been empty, now felt as hollow as a cave. Muttering fiercely, he slunk away in search of food.

As for the little squirrel, she had found her first food-store – or at least the fox had. She ran down the tree and quickly gathered up as many nuts as she could carry.

The squirrel never did find all her stores, but the nuts she hid and lost grew into new nut-trees, so they fed her daughters and her granddaughters. And they were *much* better at remembering things, I'm happy to say.

Good
Neighbours

Ruddington Bunny lived a quiet life. Every morning, after breakfast, he tidied his house. Then he read the newspaper. Sometimes he played chess with his friend Ashby Squirrel. In the afternoon, he did his shopping. And in the evening, there was nothing Ruddington liked better than a cup of blackberry tea by the fire, and a good book to read.

Ruddington enjoyed his life.
Everything about it seemed
absolutely perfect – until the day
Scarrington Owl moved into the
house just above Ruddington's.

Oh, Scarrington was friendly
enough. And he was kind and
generous and kept his house
tidy. He was a good neighbour. In
fact, thought Ruddington,
Scarrington Owl would have
been a perfect neighbour if it
hadn't been for one thing.

Scarrington was *noisy*!

Every night, just about the
time Ruddington was getting
ready for bed, Scarrington Owl
was just waking up. And when

Ruddington was snuggled down under the covers, all set to drift off to dreamland, Scarrington began to hoot.

"Hoo-hoo-hooooo," Scarrington hooted. "Hoo-hoo-HOOOOO! Hoo-hoo-HOOOOOO-hoooo-hoo!" On and on it went, all through the night. Poor Ruddington tossed and turned and just couldn't get any sleep at all.

"I'll have to do something," Ruddington muttered one night. Wearily, he stumbled out of bed and went to the window.

"Please keep your voice down," he shouted out of the open window.

But Scarrington was hooting so loudly, he didn't hear.

In desperation, Ruddington went to his broom cupboard and got out his long-handled mop. Ruddington banged the mop handle hard against the ceiling. BANG! BANG! BANG! Scarrington hooted even louder.

"I'll have to go up there myself," muttered Ruddington, putting on his dressing gown as quickly as he could.

So upstairs Ruddington Bunny climbed, and he knocked on Scarrington's door.

"Excuse me," he said, when Scarrington answered his knock, "but it's two in the morning, and I'm *trying* to get to sleep. Do you think you could hoot just a little less loudly?"

"Oh dear," said Scarrington. "I'm ever so sorry for the disturbance. I'll try to keep the noise down."

"Thank you," said Ruddington, stumbling back downstairs. He was so tired that he was almost asleep before he got back into his bed.

For the next two nights, Scarrington's hooting was a bit softer, and Ruddington thought his sleepless nights were a thing of the past. But on the third night, the hooting got louder, and on the fourth night, it was louder still. By the end of the week, things were just as bad as they ever were.

"I'm sorry," said Scarrington, when Ruddington came to see him again. "Owls just *have* to hoot at night. It's what we do, and the louder we can do it, the better. I'm afraid you'll just have to put up with it. After all, we are neighbours, and neighbours have to learn to live with one another, don't they?"

When Ashby came to visit the next morning, Ruddington said, "I'm sorry, but I'm just too tired to play chess today."

"Is it your noisy neighbour again?" asked Ashby looking sympathetically at his friend.

"Yes," wailed Ruddington. "I don't know what to do!"

"Why not try wearing earmuffs to bed?" suggested Ashby. "That's what I did when the moles who live downstairs from me had triplets. The babies cried

and cried every night, but I never heard a thing."

It was worth a try, thought Ruddington. So that afternoon he went out and bought a pair of thick, fluffy earmuffs.

But a bunny needs very *big* earmuffs, and they made poor

Ruddington terribly hot and uncomfortable. In the end, he had to take them off.

One day, Ruddington's cousin Bingham Bunny came to visit.

"I once lived next door to a family of very rowdy hedgehogs," said Bingham. "I put pillows on my walls, and that muffled the noise. Maybe that would work for you, too."

So that evening, Ruddington taped some pillows to his ceiling. Bingham was right – it *did* muffle the noise, and Ruddington fell into a deep, contented sleep. But in the middle of the night, the pillows fell down. Ruddington woke with a start – and a whole mouthful of feathers!

"It's no use," Ruddington said to himself the next morning. "I will just have to move house. It's the only way I will ever have any peace and quiet again."

Ruddington was all set to go out and see if there were any houses for rent, and had started to think about just what kind of home he would be looking for, when the post came through the door. Among the circulars and the bills, there was a very fancy envelope addressed to him, and when he opened it, he was certainly most surprised.

The card inside said:

> *You are invited to*
> *a musical evening presented by*
>
> *THE OWL OPERATIC*
> *SOCIETY*
>
> *at the home of*
> *Scarrington Owl*
>
> *7:00 PM tonight   Refreshments will be served*

So, at seven o'clock precisely, Ruddington Bunny climbed the stairs to Scarrington's house. He was pleased to see that Ashby and Cousin Bingham were both there, as well as lots of other friends and neighbours. And all the owls of the forest were there, dressed in their very best outfits. There was a long table, spread with delicious things to eat and drink, and everyone seemed in a festive mood.

After a few minutes, Scarrington cleared his throat. "Ladies and gentlemen," he announced. "Please be seated. Our recital is about to begin."

Everyone sat down, and the owls gathered together at the front of the room, standing very smartly in rows.

"Hoo-hoo-hoo-hooo," sang Scarrington, to give the others the key – and the singing began.

It was magnificent! All hooting in harmony, the owls sang their way through dozens of wonderful songs. They sang slow, romantic, sentimental songs, and quick, bright, funny songs. They even sang loud songs and soft ones, happy songs and sad ones. They even took requests and sang special favourites – and everyone joined in the choruses. As the

moon rose, and stars twinkled in sky, the music of happy voices filled the forest.

Much later, as dawn broke, the singing finally came to an end, and everyone prepared to fly, scamper, shuffle and hop home. Before he left, Ruddington went up to Scarrington.

"Thank you so much for inviting me," he said. "I can't

remember when I've had so much fun! And now that I know how delightful your hooting can be, I'm sure it won't bother me any more."

"I'm glad you had a good time," said Scarrington. "And I have some special news for you."

"Oh?" said Ruddington.

"Yes," said Scarrington Owl. "There's no need for you to worry about the noise any longer. The Owl Operatic Society has found a splendid new rehearsal hall. Starting tomorrow, you'll be glad to know that we'll be practising our hooting and singing in our very own tree."

"But you're not moving away?" asked Ruddington, anxiously.

"Of course not!" exclaimed Scarrington. "This tree will always be my home."

"Oh, I'm glad," said Ruddington Bunny. "Because, you know, you've become much more than a neighbour – you're also a very special friend!"

Mrs
Jameson's
Jelly

Mrs Janice Jameson was famous for her preserves. They regularly won top prize at the Poultry and Produce Show in the neighbouring town. Her mandarin marmalade was truly exceptional. Her plum preserve was delicious. Her juniper jam received five red rosettes in a row. But it was Mrs Jameson's famous blackberry and apple jelly that really overwhelmed her public. Every jar that she made was fought over in the local shop. Visitors came from far and wide for the chance of buying the very smallest jar, and there were sometimes queues outside

Mrs Jameson's house when the telltale smell of simmering fruit wafted out of her windows.

Now Mrs Jameson was quite rightly proud of her jam-making achievements, and she enjoyed the praise of her friends and neighbours, but eventually their appreciation went to head – with rather disastrous consequences.

One day, Mrs Jameson was asked to give a lecture on preserving to the local branch of the Ladies' Luncheon Club. It was quite an honour to be asked, and Mrs Jameson felt a flutter of nervousness as she stood up to give her speech. But she need not have worried. As soon as she embarked upon her favourite subject, her anxiety left her.

Mrs Jameson gave her spell-bound audience the benefit of her expertise on Selecting Fruits, Choosing a Preserving Pan, The Art of Stirring, Pots and Their Problems, Sinking Fruit: the Sloppy Simmerer's Curse, and Lovely Labelling. She held her listeners' attention so thoroughly that she began to feel as though no problem of preserving was so great she could not solve it.

"Now I will answer questions," she said grandly. "Who would like to begin?"

One or two ladies timidly put up their hands and voiced their own little difficulties. Mrs Janice Jameson dealt with these in brisk terms. She told one lady that her fruit was substandard and advised another to give up jam-making altogether, as she clearly had not the first idea about it. Other questions were dealt with in an equally robust way, and Mrs Jameson's audience began to be a little restless. Finally, a very superior-looking lady in an enormous hat gave a little laugh.

"It's delightful to know that such quaint old-fashioned hobbies are still being practised," she said. "Of course, those of us that have important work to do simply cannot find the time for such charming pursuits – even if we wanted to."

There was something in her tone that immediately annoyed Mrs Jameson. She felt that she did work as important as any you could mention. How dare the woman in the hat use such a patronising tone?

"I'm quite sure," she replied, "that any lady who is doing truly important work will have the intelligence and dilligence to organise her time in such a way that she can pursue *any* hobby."

"But everyone has their limits, Mrs Jameson," persisted the lady in the hat in a silky voice.

"Nonsense," cried the speaker. "Such talk is for the fainthearted. Why, despite my numerous speaking engagements, I find time to make any amount of blackberry and apple jelly each and every year."

"*Any* amount?" queried the lady in the hat.

"*Any* amount," confirmed Mrs Jameson, who recognised a challenge when she heard one.

"In that case," continued her interrogator, "would you be willing to undertake to fill any empty jars that are brought to you? We would pay for your perfect preserves, of course."

"Certainly," said Mrs Jameson. She thought quickly. Every year when she came to make her jelly there was a shortage of jars. This year was likely to be no exception. It simply was not possible that local people could find so many jars that Mrs Jameson could not fill them.

Mrs Jameson smiled sweetly at the lady in the hat. "Perhaps you would like to come and watch," she said. "I'm sure you have a great deal to learn."

Oh dear, Mrs Jameson had made an enemy, and that is never a wise thing to do if you can help it. But she was very confident of her abilities. Making jelly came as naturally to Janice Jameson as sitting in front of the television does to most people. She could not wait to roll up her sleeves and go to work.

The next morning, when Mrs Jameson opened her front door, she found a cardboard box with thirty-two empty jars inside. She laughed scornfully.

"I can make thirty-two jars of jelly before breakfast," she cried, not entirely accurately.

Ten minutes later, Mrs Jameson was on the telephone to her favourite niece.

"Leonora!" she trilled. "Your services are needed. Please go out this morning and pick as many blackberries as you can find. I shall pay my usual rates."

"No problem, Aunty," said Leonora, who had heard from a friend's mother about the Great Jelly Challenge and felt sure that her money box would gain from it.

That morning, Leonora went out and picked ten whole baskets of blackberries. She knew where the juiciest berries were to be found and was careful not to scratch her hands as she picked.

Back at home, Mrs Jameson sent her husband out to pick apples from the orchard.

"Only the best ones," she warned him.

"Yes, dear," said Mr Jameson, who had endured various tasks connected to his wife's hobby over the years.

By midday, Mrs Jameson had everything she needed. It was time to begin.

For the next few hours, the kitchen was full of delicious bubbling sounds. Mrs Jameson washed and peeled. She cored and chopped, and simmered and stirred. Finally, the moment of truth arrived. Mrs Jameson put a spoonful of jelly on a cold saucer and waited to see if it would set.

"Perfect!" cried Mrs Jameson, and she set about straining her jelly into jars.

By teatime, thirty-two jars of blackberry and apple jelly were standing on the kitchen table. Thirty-two lids had been sealed, and thirty-two labels had been written (in Mr Jameson's best handwriting). Mrs Jameson felt tired but triumphant.

But next morning, when she opened her front door, she found another cardboard box of empty jars. This time there were sixty-four of them!

Mrs Jameson felt a little faint, but she was not going to give up. Summoning her troops (otherwise known as Leonora and Mr Jameson), she set to work once more. And by the end of the day, all sixty-four jars were filled, lidded and labelled.

There was no room on the kitchen table for the new batch of jam, so Mrs Jameson carefully stacked the jars back in the cardboard box they had come in. Then she wrote "This way up" in big black letters on the box to prevent a sticky accident.

You can guess what happened the next morning. Over a hundred jars stood on Mrs Jameson's doorstep. She rose to the challenge, of course, but I have to say that she did not set about jelly-making that day with her usual enthusiasm. In fact, the troops were a little jaded as well.

"I've picked all the best berries," Leonora complained.

"Then you'll have to go farther afield," said her aunt. "I can't have substandard berries in *my* jelly."

Mr Jameson protested too. "My writing hand is aching," he said. "I think I may have done it a permanent injury."

"How do you think *my* wrists feel," demanded his wife, "with all that stirring and straining? Yes, straining is the word, I can tell you. The honour of our household is at stake. We must go on!" she finished dramatically.

Mr Jameson climbed reluctantly into the apple trees again. There were very few fruits left that were worth picking.

Mrs Jameson put on a clean apron and got to work. It was very late when she finished, but every jar was filled with jelly, and it is a tribute to the tired cook's high standards that the first jar tasted just as good as the last.

Mrs Jameson went to bed, confident that there could be no more spare jars in the whole area. It simply was not possible. Still, the next morning she opened the front door very gingerly.

It was a nightmare. There must have been at least five hundred jars standing on the step. Mrs Jameson had to sit down at the bottom of the stairs. In her heart of hearts, she knew that she could not fill five hundred jars, but she telephoned her niece all the same.

"No," said Leonora. "No, no, a thousand times no!"

"Double rates?" pleaded her aunt desperately.

"No!"

"Triple?"

"No!" And Leonora rather rudely put the phone down.

Mr Jameson's reaction was much the same.

"I'm only human, dear," he said. "I can't *make* apples appear on the trees. You've done your best. After all, you're only human too."

How Mrs Janice Jameson regretted her boastful words to the Ladies' Luncheon Club. How she wished she had known, as a friend helpfully told her at least three days too late, that the lady in the hat owned the biggest jam-jar factory in the entire country. Mrs Jameson felt that she never wanted to see another jam jar in her life.

At least the local shop had plentiful supplies of blackberry and apple jelly that year, but it was the last time it was to appear on the shelves. For Mrs Janice Jameson has sold her saucepans and taken up … knitting!

The
Rabbits
and the
Oak Tree

Now there are large families, with lots of children, and there are very small families of only two people, but when it comes to rabbits, there are *enormous* families. It was just such an enormous family that had taken up residence in a home under the roots of the oldest oak tree in the forest.

By rabbit standards, the family wasn't so very big to begin with. There were Mother Rabbit and Father Rabbit with their six children. There were two sets of grandparent rabbits and three or four sisters and brothers of Mother and Father Rabbit – *and* their children. Altogether, there must have been about thirty lively little rabbits.

The oak tree had lived in the forest for hundreds of years. Its roots were thick and twisted. As soon as he saw them, Father Rabbit knew that he could dig a very fine home among those roots, and that is exactly what he did. And the oak tree didn't seem to mind.

But over the next few years, the rabbit family didn't so much grow as *explode*! The children had children, and the children's children had children. Very soon there were over two hundred rabbits living under the oldest oak tree in the forest.

Of course, some expansion had been necessary. You can't squeeze more and more rabbits into a small space (unless you are a conjuror). So Father Rabbit and his brothers and cousins and nephews dug more and more passages and rooms among the roots of the tree. I must say they did it beautifully. There were cosy little bedrooms and spacious sitting rooms. There were places for the baby rabbits to play and quiet spots where the older rabbits could sit and chat and have a little peace.

But as the months passed, the oak tree began to feel worried. It seemed that his roots were not planted so firmly in the soil as they once had been. Where once he had enjoyed feeling the breeze whistling through his leaves, now he felt uneasy and just a little bit wavering and wobbly. Winter was coming, and the oak tree dreaded the gales that sometimes rushed through the wood.

"I don't know what to do," he muttered to the much younger birch tree standing near him.

The birch tree was very flattered. It was usually she who

asked the ancient oak tree for advice. She rustled her branches and thought as hard as possible.

"I'm sure those rabbits don't mean to do you harm," she said. "The trouble is that it's not easy for a tree to talk to a rabbit. They just don't speak the same kind of language. What you need is an interpreter. Someone who can understand both sides."

"By Jove, you're right!" cried the oak tree. "And there is only one woodland creature who can do such a thing. We need to find a woodsprite."

You have probably never seen a woodsprite, for they are so

small and flit about so quickly
that the best you can usually do
is to *think* you've caught sight of
one out of the corner of your
eye. If you have ever noticed a
leaf waving more vigorously than
its neighbours, or seen the
sunshine sparkling on a drop of
water as it shimmers on a
cobweb, you have probably
almost seen a woodsprite. They
are very difficult to find.

Luckily, ancient trees know a
little of the old magic. The oak
tree gave a kind of a rumble and
little bit of a creak. It almost
sounded as if it was singing. In
fact, it was calling to the

woodsprites to come to its aid.

In only a few moments, a little creature flitted across the clearing to the oak tree. It could have been a dried leaf, drifting in the breeze. It could have been a butterfly, alighting on a branch. It could have been a clump of fluffy dandelion seeds, floating through the air. But it wasn't. It was a woodsprite, answering the call of the mighty oak tree.

It did not take the tree long to explain the problem.

The woodsprite nodded her head and flitted down one of the holes at the base of the tree. She travelled through tunnel after

tunnel, until, as luck would have it, she came face to face with Father Rabbit, who was munching his dinner.

"Hello," said the rabbit politely. "How can I help you?"

"I'm very much afraid that you are damaging the mighty oak above you," said the woodsprite, in a voice that was no louder than a feather falling on to a bed of moss.

"Damaging it? How?" asked the rabbit in surprise. "I thought he quite liked us living here. We feel so safe among his strong roots."

"That's just the problem," explained the woodsprite. "Your

burrows have loosened the roots so much that the oak tree fears the next strong wind could cause him to fall.

"Well," said the rabbit slowly, "I don't mean to sound uncaring, but all trees must fall sometime, and the oak tree has reached a very great age."

"And could reach an even greater one," said the woodsprite. "And what do you think will happen if the tree *does* fall? Its roots will come tearing out of the ground, destroying your home and leaving your burrows open, so that any passing fox or owl could carry off your little ones."

"When you put it like that," said the rabbit, "I can see that it is our duty to help the noble tree. But it seems to me that the only way we can help is to move altogether, and leave our beautiful home."

"No, no," said the sprite. "Not ten minutes from here is a lovely patch of heath, with sandy soil and thorny bushes above. It is the perfect spot for you to dig a new home, and you will be much safer there. And if you fill in most of the burrows in this home, you could keep a smaller, holiday home here to visit in turns whenever you need a break."

That sounded an excellent idea, so the rabbit hopped off to call a family meeting to discuss the matter.

A couple of hours later, the oak tree felt a squiggly, wriggly feeling around his roots, as the rabbits started to fill in a large number of their burrows and bedrooms. Before nightfall, the tree felt much happier than he had done for weeks. His roots gripped the soil firmly, and he could allow his branches to wave without feeling that he was about to topple over. He gave a happy sigh and settled down to grow for another five hundred years or so.

Meanwhile, the rabbits were having a wonderful time in the sandy heath. In fact, they enjoyed it so much that they very soon had no wish at all to visit their holiday home under the oak tree.

So do the burrows stand empty, filling up gradually with dried leaves? No, someone has moved in who flits so lightly along the passageways that the oak tree feels his toes are being tickled. Next time you hear an oak tree giggle, don't be surprised. It is simply that a woodsprite is not far away.

The Imprisoned Princess

Long ago there lived a Princess who was good, and kind, and beautiful. She was loved by everyone who knew her.

The Princess was an only child. She would inherit the kingdom after her father the King. Although the whole country was very happy at the thought of so gracious a Queen ruling them in due course, one person schemed and plotted every day to make sure that the day of the Princess's coronation never arrived.

It was the King's sister, Lady Eldred. She also had one child, a pale boy called Ghent. She was determined that he, not the Princess, would succeed to the royal throne.

Now Lady Eldred had tried for years to show the Princess in a bad light, but she only ever succeeded in making herself look silly. When she was at her wits' end, she decided to call on greater powers than her own. She went to visit the Witch of the Wood, a woman so evil and cold that leaves shrivelled on the trees as she passed. Even Lady Eldred felt a shiver of fear as she approached the witch's lair, but she knew that she had too much to lose to turn back.

At the sound of footsteps on the woodland path, the Witch of the Wood emerged. She cackled horribly and nodded her hideous head at her visitor.

"I know why you have come, my lady," she hissed, "and I am pleased to see you." Little Miss Princess Perfect has long been gnawing at my heart. Such goodness should not be allowed to exist. I will be only too happy to help to extinguish it."

"She will need to be done away with altogether," said Lady Eldred. "She has too high a place in people's hearts now to be toppled from her throne. What did you have in mind? I will help you all I can."

"No, no, my dear," laughed the witch, "you will *pay* me all you can. I will handle the magic by myself. Although her spirit is too strong for me to take her life, the Princess can still be captured. I will imprison her inside a tree at the heart of the wood. She will stay there for ever. Your boy can become King, and the people will forget all about the sweet-as-sugar Princess."

"That is just what I wish," said Lady Eldred. "I will bring the Princess into the wood tomorrow. You can do your worst then."

The next day was bright and sunny. It was not difficult for Lady Eldred to persuade her niece to walk with her through the lovely shade of the nearby wood. They left the castle together before midday.

When they had wandered for several hours beneath the green boughs, the Princess suggested that they should return home. But they had not yet reached the witch's lair, so Lady Eldred begged her niece to follow just one more woodland path.

"Ahaaah!" cried the Witch of the Wood, leaping across their path. "One of you two ladies

must pay with her life for walking in my woodland. Which one is it to be?"

The Princess at once rushed forward to save her aunt. Her kind heart had only one wish – to protect those she loved.

"So," hissed the witch, "you have made your choice."

Her gnarled old fingers flew into the air like bats and hovered over the Princess's head. As the spell was said, the Princess's body changed. Rough bark grew around it, while the tendrils of her hair became branches and leaves. Soon not even her loving father would have recognised her. Only her spirit, too strong for the witch's power, remained free, throwing a golden glow around the tall and stately tree she had become.

The Lady Eldred returned to the castle in tears.

"I begged her not to stray from the path," she said, "but she would not listen. One moment I could see her. The next she was gone. I searched and searched, but I could not find the Princess."

At once the King sent out all his men to comb the forest for the missing girl. But although they searched every pathway and clearing, and passed several times under the branches of a particularly beautiful tree at the very heart of the wood, they returned to the castle without their master's daughter.

For weeks, the King hoped that his child would be returned to him, happy and well, but as time passed, he had to agree with his people that she had probably been dragged away by a wild animal. He knew that he would probably never see her again.

Meanwhile, something strange was happening in the wood. The Princess's spirit, hovering over her imprisoned body, warmed the trees around it. The whole woodland became so filled with sunshine and warmth that the witch's presence was much easier to spot. Around her lair, the trees shrivelled and died. Wherever she walked through the forest, the moss blackened beneath her feet, and trees shed their leaves as though winter was on its way.

Working in the wood, there was a young woodcutter. He noticed the changes among the trees and realised at once that something evil was lurking there. But he saw other trees flourish and turn their faces to the light, so he knew that something very valuable had come into the woodland as well.

Then, one day, the woodcutter noticed a tree he had never seen before. It was so beautiful that it took his breath away, and it made him feel at once happy and sad. He longed to stay beside it for ever, and laughed at himself for feeling so strongly about a tree that his work would one day cause him to cut down.

Nevertheless, the woodcutter spent as much time near the tree as he possibly could. One day, as he sat beneath its branches, eating his lunchtime bread and cheese, a little breeze danced through the leaves. It was as though the tree was speaking to him. "*Free me. Free me,*" it breathed. "*Free me. Free me.*"

The woodcutter sprang to his feet. "How?" he cried. "I will do anything, anything at all."

The tree spoke no more, but it came into the woodcutter's mind what he must do. He must cut down the beautiful tree!

For a long time, the young man resisted the idea. He could not bear to destroy something so lovely, but the voice in his head insisted. He knew that he would have no peace until he had carried out the dreadful act.

With tears in his eyes, the woodcutter swung his axe. It sank with a horrible thud into the body of the tree. Tears were streaming down the young man's face as he worked on. Over and over, the silvery blade of his axe swung through the air. At last, with a heartrending shriek, the tree fell to the ground – and a beautiful girl seemed to rise from its ruins.

It was the Princess, freed from the witch's spell.

"So much of the witch's magic was holding me in the tree," she explained. "I knew that if the tree was killed, she too would die."

The woodcutter looked around him. The moss that had been black was fresh and green again. The trees that had shrivelled were putting out new shoots and reaching towards the sky.

"I think she is dead," he said, "but how did you survive?"

"I was not thinking of myself," said the Princess gently, "perhaps that is why the witch's death freed me as well. Whatever the reason, I have a very great deal to thank you for."

"Let me take you safely to your home," said the woodcutter, taking the Princess's hand. "There is no need to thank me."

But somewhere along the woodland path, the Princess realised that she wished never to part from the handsome young man, and he had fallen just as much in love with her.

The King was so overjoyed to see his lost daughter again that he hardly blinked when she told him she was about to marry a woodcutter.

"Splendid!" he said. "It's time there was some new blood in our family tree. Oh, I say, did you hear that? A woodcutter in a family tree! That's rather funny."

Chuckling at his own joke, the King led the happy couple to the

Great Hall, where Lady Eldred sat
sewing by the fire, dreaming of
the crown that would one day sit
upon the head of her son.

At the sight of the Princess,
Lady Eldred rose to her feet. The
colour flooded from her face,
and she would have fallen, if the
King had not put out a hand to
catch her.

"It is a shock, isn't it?" he said. "But such a happy one. How glad you must be to see your lost niece again."

But for the first time in her life, Lady Eldred showed her true colours. All the hatred she had felt for the Princess came tumbling out of her mouth. Even her son was pale with disgust.

So it was that Lady Eldred watched the festivities for the marriage of her niece from the tower in which she had been imprisoned. She felt that the wheel had turned full circle, for as the daughter of a King, she too was an imprisoned Princess.

The First
Christmas
Tree

On a very special night, long, long ago, a star shone down upon a stable. Night after night, it shone, until some wise men, travelling from the East, reached the building over which it hovered. They went inside to offer gifts of gold, frankincense and myrrh to the baby they found inside.

Later, the baby and its parents were warned of danger, and they packed their belongings in the night and journeyed on to Egypt.

Few people know that the star also continued on its travels, wandering across the dark sky in search of a final resting place.

The star travelled over the desert, and looked down on mile upon mile of barren sand. As the winds blew, the sand was constantly shifted from place to place, forming mountains and valleys that were never still. That was no place for a star to rest.

As the star journeyed, it crossed the ocean. Far below, the restless waves were in ceaseless motion. Over and over again, they rose and fell, for the ocean is never at peace. The star could not find a final stopping place on the restless seas.

The star travelled on, and many people looked up into the night sky and pointed at the shining visitor.

"What does it mean? Will it bring us good luck or bad?" they asked each other.

But the star carried no luck. It simply shone by night and became dark by day, always travelling to find a place to stay.

The star travelled over the mountains, as cold and bright in the moonlight as the star itself. On their peaks, the snow lay unchanging, but on the slopes below, it sometimes drifted into heaps and sometimes melted into a fast-flowing river, gushing down the rocky mountain face to the valleys beneath. Even the unchanging mountains endlessly shifted and shrugged, sometimes sending down huge shelves of snow as avalanches. The star could not rest on a mountain top.

On its journey, the star travelled over towns and cities, where lights burned as brightly by night as they did by day. In the orange glow given off by a thousand lamps and candles, the star could hardly be seen. It could not come to rest in such a place as that.

When it came to the great empty wastes of the Arctic, the star believed that it had found a home as pure and changeless as itself. It hovered above the North Pole and saw itself reflected far below in the great sheets of ice that cover the sea. Everything was cold, cold and silent. The star looked down on the earth and felt disconnected and alone. It found that what it sought was peace, not emptiness.

Moving south again, the star came to a great forest. In the moonlight, its trees seemed

clothed in dark green robes. Here and there, frost sugared their branches, and tiny creatures huddled to keep warm. The trees were majestic, straight and tall, and they were growing. With every second that passed, the trees were reaching higher and higher, slowly stretching nearer and nearer to the star. For a long time, the star hovered over the forest, not knowing where to come to rest.

Then, far below, it saw that the trees were beginning to thin. Further south, they did not stand in serried ranks but grew singly, tall and proud. One tree in particular seemed to stand as a bridge between the earth and sky, its roots firmly in the soil, while its topmost branches brushed the stars.

The special star floated gently above the mighty tree, so that its pure, white light lay cleanly upon the feathery branches. This was the place where it would stay, in touch with all above and below.

At Christmas time, when we remember the baby in the stable and the star that shone, night after night, above the poor building, many people bring a fir tree into their homes and place a silver star at its very top. It is a reminder that the star of the first Christmas, although it was far too high and heavenly to be reached by people on earth, still shed light into their lives, and came to rest with all the living things here below.

A
Woodland
Home

When Thistledown the elf decided to move out of his parents' home in the trunk of a tree, he knew just what he was looking for. He had always liked the idea of living in a toadstool house. Some elves these days think that those red and white dwellings are gaudy and not in the best possible taste, but Thistledown thought he would feel like a grown-up elf if he lived in one. The only problem was finding the right property.

Elves do not really have estate agents, but they do have homefinders, who usually know what kinds of houses are available in the local area. Young Thistledown trotted along to see the nearest friendly homefinder straight away.

"What kind of property are you looking for?" asked the plump homefinder, making notes on an official-looking clipboard.

Thistledown explained how much he liked toadstool houses.

"Then I have just the right thing for you!" exclaimed the homefinder. "Come along with me right now, for it will be in great demand."

The homefinder, whose name was Locket, led Thistledown deep into the wood, where some of the trees were old and rotten, while others had fallen and lay across the paths.

"It's not a very fashionable neighbourhood," said the young elf, looking about him.

"It is very competitively priced to take account of that," said Locket severely, "and the price you are prepared to pay is ... well ... shall we say *modest*?"

Thistledown felt that he had been put firmly in his place, but he was a sensible young elf and kept an open mind about the house he was going to see.

At last, Locket stood still and gestured dramatically.

"Here you are!" he said. "As you can see, it is part of a terrace of three homes."

Thistledown looked carefully at the very fine toadstools standing at the base of an old tree. He rubbed his eyes and looked again.

"But there are no doors or windows!" he cried.

Locket consulted his clipboard. "As it says here," he said, "these toadstools are absolutely *ripe* for conversion."

But Thistledown shook his head vigorously.

"No," he said. "I am definitely looking for something that I can move into right away. And I really do think that I should like to live in a better part of the wood. I wouldn't want my visitors to be worried about being attacked by owls when they came to see me. Besides, it's very dark here. I'd like to see the sunshine from time to time. That is essential."

Locket hugged his clipboard to his chest.

"I can see that you are going to be a very demanding client," he said, "but it's my job to find you what you are looking for. There is another house I'd like you to see. It's not exactly a toadstool, but I think you will find it full of traditional charm."

Thistledown wasn't at all sure what this meant, but it turned out to be the way that Locket described a damp, dark, tree-root house very near to the rejected unconverted toadstools.

"No," said Thistledown. "This isn't what I am looking for at all."

Over the next few days, Locket took Thistledown to see over thirty possible places. All of them, in Thistledown's view, were absolutely dreadful. There was a tree-trunk house that was so ramshackle a great chunk of bark came off in his hand. There was a toadstool house that a family of black beetles had already occupied. Thistledown had a particular horror of black beetles, ever since one of them had crawled into his acorn bed when he was a baby. There was also a disused bird's nest, which had fallen to the ground, a tiny cave that looked as if it would

get flooded whenever it rained,
and a little cottage with no roof.

"That is the last property I
have to show you," said Locket.
"I wonder if you are being quite
realistic about your requirements,
young man. When it comes to
choosing a home, you do
sometimes have to compromise."

Thistledown said that he quite
understood about compromise,
but he really couldn't live in
anything he had so far seen.

"I'll know it when I see it," he
said of his dream home. "And
then I won't hesitate, believe me."

Thistledown's parents were
secretly very happy that their

son had not yet found a suitable house. They did not really want him to move out.

"When you have saved up some more, it will be easier," said his father. "It's always hard setting up home for the first time. I remember it well."

"You weren't by yourself," retorted Thistledown's mother. "You were already married to me, and we would never have found our first home if it had been left up to you!" She winked at Thistledown. "You follow your dream, son," she said. "There are plenty of people who will try to persuade you to settle for second best. Don't you listen to them, will you?"

So Thistledown continued to look at possible homes, and he continued to be disappointed. As the weeks passed, he became more and more depressed.

"Perhaps it would be better if you found a home of your own, if this is how you're going to be," said his father unsympathetically, when Thistledown had mooched into the house in a miserable way for the fourth time that week.

"That's exactly the trouble," muttered Thistledown.

The next day, however, he really did try to pull himself

together. He decided to take himself off for a long walk, to clear his head and raise his plunging spirits.

In fact, it was a beautiful day. The sun sparkled through the leaves, and little woodland animals were scampering and chattering wherever he looked. It was the kind of day on which it felt good to be an elf, and young Thistledown began to feel better. What was he complaining about? He already had a safe, warm home, where he was welcome to stay as long as he needed. One day, he would find the home of his own that he was dreaming about, and until that day came, things were really not so bad.

Thistledown breathed in the warm, woodland air. He kicked his heels in the clearings and twizzled around the trees. Then, quite suddenly, he saw something that made his heart stand still. It was a perfect toadstool house.

Thistledown stood with his mouth open for a moment. The little house was exactly what he had imagined. It had two little windows and a tiny door. Its roof was red and white, just as toadstool roofs should be.

As Thistledown stood there, staring at the little house, the door opened, and a very pretty elfin girl came out to shake crumbs from a tablecloth. She saw Thistledown at once and smiled at him.

"Can I help you?" she asked. "Were you looking for someone?"

"Yes, no, yes!" said the young elf.

"Well, which is it?" laughed the girl, folding her tablecloth.

"I was looking for a something, not a someone," said the elf.

"What sort of a something?" The girl looked puzzled.

"A house!" cried Thistledown. "Your house is the most beautiful I have ever seen."

"Well, thank you," said the girl, looking a little pink. "I am very fond of it myself. It was given to me by my favourite aunt, who had to move away. I'm very lucky to own such a lovely home."

Then Thistledown found himself telling the girl all about his own quest. She was amazingly easy to talk to, and before long, she had invited

Thistledown in to have some dandelion tea.

Over the next few days, the young elf's parents noticed that his step became lighter and his smile came more easily. It was not long before he introduced them to the reason for his happiness and told them that he and his new friend had decided they would like to get married.

So although Thistledown is now living in his dream home, he does not think it's the most important thing in the world. In looking for a something, he *did* find a someone, and that is better than anything.

The
King of the
Forest

Once upon a time, there was a King who loved trees. Ever since he was a baby Princeling, when his nurse put him out in his crib to look up at the green leaves of a mighty oak waving above him, he had loved all living things. But trees made his heart sing and his eyes grow misty. He thought they were the most beautiful things in the world.

When he was a boy, the King climbed every tree he could find. From high in the branches, he could almost feel that he was part of the tree, swaying in the wind, warm in the summer sunshine. He wished that he

could live there for ever, and
often spent the night in a little
treehouse built for him by the
Royal Carpenter. There he could

forget he was a Prince and pretend to be like other children. For Princes are brought up to know that they will one day have the terrible responsibility of being King. Some Princes cannot wait to sit upon the throne, but others long for a quiet life, doing the things they love.

The hero of this story was just like that. If he had had his way, he would have stayed all day among his beloved trees, far away from the busy world of life at court.

However, the day came, as everyone expected, when the old King died. The new King wept for his father and for himself, for he felt that his freedom was over.

No longer could the new King wander in the woods he loved. He had to sit in his palace, reading documents and listening to the requests of his subjects.

Not all of the work was boring. The King enjoyed helping people who needed his aid, and some of the pageants and processions were very impressive, but he had no time to walk beneath the shady boughs or tend the oak trees around the palace.

One day, however, as he looked at an ancient map of his kingdom, he noticed a large area of green at the very edge of his realm.

"What is that?" he asked his Chief Minister.

"That, Sire, is an ancient wood, planted by your great-great-great-great-great-great-great-great grandfather. Most of it has been cut down now, which is why you do not see it on more modern maps of our beloved country."

"So when you say my great-great-whatever planted it...," the King began.

"Of course, Sire, I mean that he instructed that it should be planted. He didn't go out there himself. Ha ha! No, no, royal workers planted the trees under royal instructions."

The King felt happier than he had at any time since he came to the throne.

"This," he said, "is a custom that I feel is worth reviving. We shall plant a new royal forest, and it will bigger and better than any forest ever planted."

Despite his busy workload, over the next few months, the King somehow managed to find time to supervise every detail of

the plans for the new forest. It was going to be magnificent.

"I should like planting to begin immediately," he said, when the site had been chosen. "Send the Chief Forester to me."

But the Chief Forester looked very worried when the King outlined his plans.

"I don't think that will be possible, Sire," he said.

"Not possible?" cried the King. "Why ever not? We have the men. We have the land."

"But we don't have the plants, Sire," said the Chief Forester. "We will need thousands and thousands, no, probably millions and millions of little oak tree plants, and there are not that number to be had in this kingdom or the next. Indeed, I am sure that there are not so many baby trees of the right kind to be found in the whole world."

The King paused. There was no doubt in his mind that his Chief Forester was absolutely right. Why had he not thought of it before? Would his great plan have to be abandoned after all?

"Let me think about it," said the King, "and come to see me at the same time tomorrow. This will be an extraordinary forest. We shall need an extraordinary plan."

All night long, the King tossed and turned. He was determined that his forest would be planted.

"I need this forest," he muttered to himself. "The people need this forest. The King's forest. The people's forest. *The people's forest!*" That was it! The King fell into a deep and peaceful sleep.

Next morning, the King could hardly wait for his Chief Forester to arrive. When he did, the King explained his plan. The Forester's eyes widened, but he was smiling. It would work!

Losing no time, the King called for a proclamation to be sent to every part of his realm.

ALL SUBJECTS

are invited to

*PLANT AN
ACORN*

for the Royal Forest

Full instructions given.

*Your tree could live for a
thousand years!*

It was a wonderful idea. There was hardly a person in the kingdom who didn't plant a little acorn in a pot, or a jar, or a cup. Tiny children of two years old planted them. Venerable old gentlemen of ninety-two planted them. All anybody could talk about, wherever you went, was how well their acorns were growing. The newspapers gave advice on the best growing conditions. Magazines devoted whole articles to the best way to talk to your acorn, for one of the greatest gardeners in the land had announced that all plants do better if they are talked to regularly. Another magazine suggested songs that could be sung to the acorns, while yet another actually asked a composer to write a special acorn song.

Soon, little shoots began to appear, then two little leaves. After two years, sturdy little oak tree plants stood on the doorstep of every house in the land.

At last, the Great Planting could begin.

It took five hundred men a whole year to plant the forest. After that, a hundred men tended the small plants and watched them grow into slender saplings.

Well, that was long ago, but the forest still stands. Now, not only the King but all his people can walk proudly under the majestic trees and say to their children, "Your great-great-great-great grandfather (or grandmother!) planted one of these trees."

The people love the forest almost as much as the King who planted it. Although he died long ago, he is remembered by everyone in the country as the King of the Forest. If he is looking down on it now, he will be weeping for joy – or making plans for another forest of his beloved oak trees!

The
Last Tree

Once upon a time, there was an island covered with trees. They grew so thickly that their branches met overhead. No light from the sun could filter down to the forest floor, so nothing grew there. And as nothing grew except trees, there was also nothing for most small animals and insects to eat. Only a few creatures survived in the topmost branches of the trees, where the sunlight dappled the glossy green leaves.

One day, a scientist came to the island. He examined the trees and the living things that shared the island with them. Then he sent in his report to the ruler of the country that owned the island.

The scientist reported that trees had overrun the island, destroying other plant life and severely restricting the wildlife that could survive there. He advised that exactly half of the trees should be cut down. This would allow light to reach the forest floor. Gradually, other species would begin to thrive again on the island.

The ruler to whom the report was sent hesitated. He formed several committees to discuss the matter. He set up a special enquiry to look at other parts of the world where similar actions had been taken. He asked another scientist to prepare his own report, to check the findings of the first scientist.

At last, the ruler found that the advice he was receiving from everyone was overwhelming. He ordered that half the trees on the island should be cut down.

It took a long while for the work to be carried out. There was nowhere on the island that the woodcutters could so much as pitch a tent, so they had to travel to the island each day in a boat. They had only a few hours to work before the boat returned to take them back home to the mainland before nightfall.

When the woodcutters had finished their work, all the fallen trees had to be removed. Once again committees, special enquiries and two scientists suggested suitable methods. In the end, it was a small boy, who had been reading his sister's encyclopedia, who offered the solution. The trees were pushed into the sea and floated on the tide to the mainland.

For several years, no one visited the island. The plan was to leave it undisturbed to see what new kinds of plants and animals would begin to live there. Finally, after seven years, the original scientist returned to the island.

It was a terrible disappointment. Instead of leaving space for new plants to grow, the felling of the trees had given the remaining trees extra space to grow taller themselves. Their branches grew longer, until they touched each other overhead. Just as before, not a single ray of sunlight reached the forest floor. Only the creatures that had survived before the trees were cut down still lived on the island, high in the branches.

The ruler demanded that new studies and new committees should be set up. Another plan was needed for the island. It didn't seem to occur to anyone that the island could simply be left alone.

This time, the advice was more sweeping. All the trees must be cut down to enable other living things to grow on the island.

After the usual committees and enquiries, the plan was carried out. Once again, it was a mammoth task. In fact, this time, the trees were bigger and more difficult to fell. When every single tree was cut down, they were floated away to the nearby mainland as before.

Another seven years passed before a study was carried out. This time, two scientists visited the island together. As they approached it in their boat, they peered at the horizon, looking for signs of life – a fuzz of green over the island, perhaps, or the beating of wings as a flock of birds rose up at their approach. But they found nothing.

That's right. There were no trees. No birds. No insects. No plants. No animals. There were no living things on the island at all. It was dead.

The scientists spent two days searching for even the tiniest sign of life. Finally, they were forced to admit that even seaweed did not grow on the rocks around the shore.

Something had plainly gone wrong. The ruler set up a committee as usual, to find out where mistakes had been made.

On the last day of the enquiry, a very important witness came to give his opinion.

This old man was well known as a world authority on islands and the living things that make their homes on them. He was rather frail now, but his mind was as sharp as ever. Everyone waited with interest for his views.

"Is it a fact," he was asked, "that no living things now survive on the island?"

"Yes, that is true," he replied.

"And is it a fact that there are no living things *able* to survive on the island?"

"No," he said, "that is not so."

"So what are these creatures or plants that could do well on so barren a piece of ground?"

The old man looked around at everyone in the room.

Why, trees," he said.

The Wize
Wizard

There was once a wizard who lived deep in a forest. His life was very lonely. The only people he ever saw were travellers, journeying through the forest on their way to somewhere else.

The wizard looked forward to these meetings. He preferred to live on his own, but it was nice to see a friendly face sometimes. In winter, when the paths were clogged with snow, and travelling was hard, he often did not see a soul for three months together.

One winter's night, when the wind howled around his windows, and a nasty draught was sneaking through the

floorboards, the wizard heard an urgent knock on the door.

At first, he ignored it, assuming that it was the branch of a tree or one of the other woodland sounds that come on a windy night. But the hammering came again, and this time there was no doubt about.

The wizard was very surprised. Surely the weather was much too bad for anyone to be out on a night like this?

The wizard went to the door and opened it just a crack, not because he was worried about who might be outside, but to stop the wind howling into his home and blowing his papers from this week to next.

But as soon as the wizard had unlatched the door, it was pushed roughly open, and a menacing figure in furs and skins strode into the room, as the icy wind blasted past him and flurries of snow blew up around the open doorway.

By instinct, the wizard pushed the door shut again before he turned to his visitor. He did not feel afraid, but he certainly was wary and careful in what he said.

"My name is Eyebright," he said. "May I have the honour of knowing your name?"

The stranger growled. "It's none of your business," he said. "Give me something to eat."

The wizard looked carefully at the man. He could see that he had lived a rough life that had furrowed his brow and greyed his hair. He looked half dead with cold, and there was a paleness about his skin that made the wizard wonder if he was well.

The wizard also noticed that the visitor carried both a sword and a mighty axe, hanging from his belt. He had no doubt that the man would not hesitate to use them, so he went to his store cupboard and brought out bread and cheese. Then he filled a bowl with soup that had been bubbling on the stove, and put it before the hungry man.

The man ate as if he had not seen food for weeks, as indeed he had not. When he had finished, he lay back in his chair, exhausted, although the wizard noticed that he kept one hand on his axe handle at all times.

"Have you been travelling long?" asked the wizard.

"None of your business," replied the stranger again. And he promptly fell right off the chair and collapsed on to the floor. His eyes were closed, and his breath came shallowly, as the wizard bent over him.

Eyebright could see that his first guess had been right. It was not simply cold and starvation that ailed the man. Gingerly, the wizard pulled off the sick man's great fur cloak. He gasped when he saw the deep wound in the stranger's shoulder.

Now Eyebright was not the kind of wizard who does spectacular spells or makes himself disappear. He was an everyday sort of wizard, who knew a great deal about wild plants and herbs and the movement of the stars. He had studied for years to learn the secrets of living things and the world around him. As a result, he was a very wise man.

For two months, the wizard looked after the man who had come in from the storm. During that time, the man was hardly ever conscious. In his dreams, he mumbled about battles fought and chances taken. The wizard was not at all sure that he could save the stranger's life.

Very gradually, however, the man improved. His sleep became quieter, and his head tossed less violently upon the pillow. The wound in his shoulder was healing slowly, and the spoonfuls of soup that the wizard had patiently dripped between his lips had given him new strength.

One day, watery sunshine flooded into the wizard's home. Outside his door, he picked the first small bunch of snowdrops and put it in a little pot by the stranger's bed. For the first time, the man opened his eyes and seemed to understand what he could see. As his gaze fell upon the delicate white flowers, his lips trembled into a tiny smile.

But as the man stared around, his fierce manner returned. He scowled and struggled to sit up.

"Where am I, and who are you?" he demanded, staring at the wizard's books and papers.

"I am Eyebright," explained the wizard again. "You came to me two months ago. You were cold and starving, and you had a dreadful wound in your shoulder. I have cared for you as well as I could, and I think that if you are careful, you will now recover."

The stranger was silent for a moment. "Has anyone been here?" he asked. "Who knows I am here?"

"No one," said the wizard. "The weather has been too bad for travellers to venture through the deepest parts of the forest. Now that spring is on its way, we shall see more visitors along the path."

At that, the stranger started up, wincing with pain as he staggered to his feet. He reached for his fur cloak, searching wildly for his sword and axe.

"They are here," said the wizard, holding up the weapons, "but you should not rush off so quickly. You still need rest and time for your shoulder to heal properly. If you go now, I cannot guarantee that all will be well."

With a great howl, the man leapt at the wizard, wrenching the sword and axe from his grasp and hurling him to the floor. Then he dropped to his knees and held the blade of the sword across the wizard's throat.

"If you tell anyone I have been here," he said, "I will come back one dark night and kill you. Or shall I finish you now?"

There was a long moment of silence as the sharp sword blade dug into Eyebright's throat. At first the wizard could hardly breathe, he was so frightened. Then he looked into the angry stranger's eyes and began, very softly, to speak.

"You are a brave man," he said. "From your appearance and the few words I understood you to say while you were ill, I take it that you are a soldier. That is something to be proud of. So, I must ask you, my friend, what are you afraid of?"

For a split second, fury rose in the stranger's eyes, then he released the wizard and pulled himself slowly to his feet. He let his sword drop on the floor and moved painfully over to a chair.

"Your words have pierced my heart," he said. "I am not a soldier, friend, I am a brigand. I make my living by stealing from travellers in the forest. I have killed men, and I have robbed those who could not afford to lose so much as a halfpenny. Oh, I was a soldier once, but I lost one battle after ten years of fighting for my King, and I was punished. After that, my heart became bitter. No one showed kindness to me, and I showed mercy to no one … until I met you. There is a price on my head. Sooner or later someone will kill me for my price, and that is all that I deserve."

The wizard smiled at the stranger. "And do you plan to continue in your old life, when you leave here?" he asked, pouring a drink for the visitor.

"No," said the man, "for my heart is no longer in it. You have reminded me of the way I used to live, trying to do what is right, helping people where I could. I cannot go back to stealing and killing now. But it is too late for me. The next traveller to pass will recognise me for sure, and it will all be over. The King's men will cut me down."

"You are too weak to travel at the moment," said the wizard, "but I feel sure that you could make a new life for yourself in another country. In the meantime, I think I know how we can make sure that no passer-by recognises you."

And that is why, when travellers stopped for a drink and crust of bread at the wizard's door that spring, they found the wizard seemed taller and stronger in his robes, though he was as kindly and welcoming as ever.

In midsummer, the wizard and the brigand parted company. No

one would have recognised the clean-shaven man in forest green who strode along the path towards a new life.

The wizard watched him go with a smile. Then he went back to his quiet and sometimes lonely ways. To this day, he is wise enough to see some goodness in everyone he meets, and somehow, that means that there is simply more goodness to go around.

The Woodman's Daughter

Once upon a time, there lived a hardworking woodman. All day he was busy in the forest, trimming and felling trees. Once a week, he would load up his cart with wood and set off for the nearest town to sell it. It was a long and tiring journey, and the woodman rarely arrived home before darkness had fallen.

When the woodman was very young, he met a pretty girl on one of his trips to the town. She thought him strong and handsome, and he was bowled over by her loveliness. For a whole year, they met once a week, and both began to long for the days to pass until their next precious meeting.

At last, the woodman plucked up the courage to ask the girl to marry him. To his delight, she agreed, and her father was only too delighted to welcome the hardworking young man into his large family.

"It is a pity you have no brothers!" he joked, looking at his eight remaining daughters.

The wedding was a simple affair, for neither the woodman nor his father-in-law had much money, but you have never seen a happier couple than the pair who left the church together.

If only it had lasted! At first all went well. The newly married couple were only unhappy when they were parted. But the wife began to realise that she must be on her own all day in the lonely forest. She was used to the town, where she could visit her friends or look in shop windows when she was bored. Here there was nothing but trees. The young wife soon began to feel that she hated trees more than anything else on earth.

The woodman could not understand why his wife became sad and silent. He had been brought up to a life in the forest.

Nothing was more beautiful to him than an oak tree standing proudly in a glade, its branches outspread to shelter the little creatures who made their homes around it.

However, the young man understood that his wife might miss her family and her old home, so he took her with him each week when he carted his logs into town. The young woman came to long for those days, just as she had longed for them before her marriage.

Then, one day, the woodman's wife told him that she was going to have a child. The woodman was overjoyed. Not only did he long for a son to teach the ways of the woods, but he felt that his wife would be happier with someone to look after all day.

But as the time for the baby's birth drew near, the mother-to-be became more and more quiet and sullen. The woodman felt sure that it was simply that she was tired and longing for her baby to be born.

That week, when the couple went into the nearby town, everything was as usual. The woodman took his wife to her parents' house, while he went to sell his wood.

However, when he returned to collect his wife, he found her father at the door, looking worried and upset.

"I'm sorry, my son," said the old man, "but she refuses to return with you. She insists that she must stay here until the baby is born. Perhaps she is right. A woman should have other women about her at such a time. She will feel differently when it is all over."

The woodman was surprised and unhappy, but he could understand how his young wife might be feeling, so he kissed her gently and left her in the town.

Each week after that, the woodman rushed eagerly to his father-in-law's house to see his wife. And the third time he visited, he was greeted by the wonderful sound of a baby's cry.

The woodman flew upstairs to see his son. His wife was sitting up in bed, the baby beside her in a cradle. The young man hugged and kissed his wife and asked how she was. Then he turned to the cradle and looked down on the most perfect little baby he had ever seen.

"He's beautiful," he breathed, touching one tiny hand. "What shall we call him?"

"I have named her Agnes," said his wife, hardly looking at the child beside her.

The woodman was shocked. "I don't know why, but I was expecting a boy!" he cried. "Well, she is lovely too, of course. And perhaps we shall have a son next time, my dear."

But his wife turned her face away and gazed out of the window with a faraway look.

The woodman could hardly wait to take his family home again. Each week, before he set out for the town, he put flowers in all the rooms and laid the table for two.

But each week, he returned alone to the forest. At first, his wife said that she was tired and unwell from the birth. The woodman was sympathetic and told her to stay as long as she liked with her family.

Later, when his wife was up and about, she said that the baby was too delicate for the long journey. The woodman had no experience of babies. His daughter looked strong and healthy, but he could not be sure. Perhaps it was right that she should stay.

Gradually, weeks turned into months. Soon, it was almost a

year since the woodman's wife had come back to live with her family. The young man began to understand in his heart that she would never return to live with him. His little daughter would grow up outside the forest.

Each week, the woodman went to see his little girl. She seemed to wait eagerly for his visits, and put up her chubby little arms to be hugged. Now it was the woodman who looked forward to his trips to town once again. They were the highlight of his week.

Then, one day, when the woodman called at his father-in-law's house, the old man met him at the door with a look of shame on his kindly face.

"My daughter is not here," he said. "She left this note for us. It seems that she met a soldier in the town and has gone overseas with him. She slipped out one night. We did not see her go."

The woodman felt as if a knife had stabbed into his heart.

"And my little one?" he gasped.

"Oh, she is here," said the old man. "She will be so happy to see her daddy again."

The woodman ran into the house and scooped up his little daughter in his arms. The tears ran down his weatherbeaten cheeks as he thought how nearly he had lost her.

"I am taking her with me," he said. "She shall live in the forest."

The fond grandfather tried to persuade the woodman not to take the little girl, but his mind was made up.

"I will bring her to see you every week," he promised.

So the little girl went to live with her father. Every day, he took her with him into the forest, which she grew to love as dearly as her father did.

The years passed, and the little girl grew up. She was the loveliest child you have ever seen. And as time went on, she became a very beautiful young woman indeed.

Now it was the young men of the town who looked forward to the woodman's weekly visit, for his lovely daughter accompanied him. It was not long before she met a young tailor, and found that she liked him very much.

When the tailor shyly approached the woodman to ask for his daughter's hand, he was not ready for the reception he received. The normally gentle woodman threw him across the street and warned him never to come near his daughter again.

"I cannot bear to lose you," he told his daughter. "And besides, marriages between townsfolk and forestfolk never work out. You must stay at home in future."

Now the woodman did not mean to be unkind, but he was afraid, so afraid, that the girl who had become the centre of his life would be lost to him for ever. In his fear, he could not think or feel properly, and so he made his daughter a prisoner in her home.

But the young girl loved her tailor, and although she loved her father too, she felt a new life calling to her. One day, when her father was at work, she packed her bags and walked the long miles into the town. She and the tailor were married that very day.

When he discovered that his daughter was gone, the woodman was beside himself with grief. He felt that he had lost the only thing in the world that mattered to him. For the first time in his life, he did not go out into the forest, but lay on his bed and stared blankly at the ceiling. He foresaw day after day of dark loneliness stretching out ahead. It was too much to bear.

But as tears stained his pillow, the woodman heard the sound of a horse and cart growing nearer.

It was the woodman's daughter and her new husband.

When he saw his daughter's happy face, the woodman could not feel angry or sad any more.

"Forgive me," he cried. "I thought I only wanted you to be happy, but I was really only thinking of myself."

"No, no," said the girl, putting her arms around him. "I know that you were worried for me and wanted to keep me safe at home. But my husband is a good man. He will bring me to see you as often as I like, and you shall come to visit us too. We have a beautiful little house, not quite in the town and not quite in the forest, but just where the trees end and the road begins.

Now the woodman cried tears of joy. He understood that in order to keep something, you sometimes have to let it go free.

The woodman is old now. He no longer goes to the town with his logs, but he looks forward to his daughter's visits. They are the highlight of his week.

Besides, he now has a grandson who takes a great interest in the forest. The woodman is eager to teach the boy all he knows, which makes him very happy.

The
Song of
Spring

There was once a little bird who lived in a tree on the edge of a wood. All year long, she was as busy as could be. In spring, she chose a site for her new nest and gathered twigs and moss to build it. Then she laid her eggs and settled down to hatch them.

She only left the eggs for seconds at a time, when she hopped off to find a quick snack. It was during one of these very short breaks that something strange happened in the little bird's nest. When she returned, one of her eggs seemed to have grown bigger!

"That's odd," said the little bird to herself. "It has never happened before."

But the egg was the right shape and the right colour. The little bird wondered if she had become so tired sitting on the eggs that she could no longer think properly. She decided to have a quick snooze and settled down comfortably once again.

Day after day, the little bird sat on her nest, keeping the eggs snug and warm.

"Soon I shall hear that first little *tap tap*," she said to herself. "Then I shall see my darling little children. I can hardly wait."

Sure enough, the little bird woke one morning to a tiny sound under her feathers. *Tap tap! Tap tap!*

Soon a little crack appeared in one of the eggs, and a tiny orange beak poked through. It was followed by a sleepy little head and a damp little body. Then the new nestling sat quietly in the sun until his feathers dried.

The little bird hardly had time to feel proud of her son before another *tap tap!* came from one of the other eggs. Once again, a little beak was followed by a little bird. Now there were two.

The little bird had to wait until evening for her third egg to hatch. This baby was just as beautiful as the first two.

The mother bird looked at the last egg. It was the largest of all. She listened hard, but could hear no tapping. Surely this egg was not going to be much longer?

One day passed and then another. The little bird did not know what to do. She needed to fly off to find food for her three little nestlings, but she did not like to leave the unhatched egg. At last, there was a very loud *TAP TAP!* and the last egg cracked in two. Out hopped a very strange bird indeed.

The mother bird felt a thrill of fear. She knew exactly what this bird was. It was a *cuckoo*. If she was not careful, it would push her other babies out of the nest.

The baby cuckoo stared at its mother and opened its beak. It already wanted food.

"All right," said the bird, "I will feed you, but you must promise me not to harm any of my other babies. If you do, I will push *you* right out of the nest. Do you understand me?"

"*Quark!*" The young cuckoo understood very well.

That spring, the mother bird exhausted herself finding food for her brood. At last the day came when they flew away from the nest.

It was sad for the mother, but her heart swelled with pride when she heard a bird singing far away.

"*Cuckoo cuckoo!*"

"That's my boy," she said.